THIS OLD MAN

ILLUSTRATED BY CAROL JONES

Houghton Mifflin Company Boston 1990

Printed in Hong Kong

10 9 8 7 6 5 4 3 2 1

For Sally and Mark

e played . . .

ack on my . . .

D

With a nick

give a

This old man

This old man he played . . .

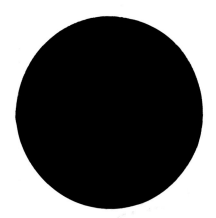

TWO

He played nick nack on my . . .

SHOE

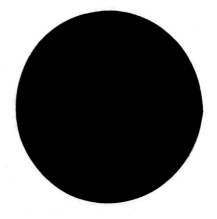

With a nick nack Paddy whack,

give a dog a bone.

This old man came rolling home.

This old man he played . . .

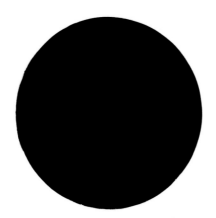

THREE

He played nick nack on my . . .

KNEE

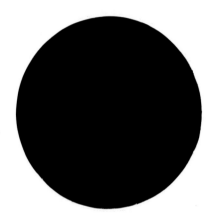

With a nick nack Paddy whack,

give a dog a bone.

This old man came rolling home.

he played . . .

VR

hack on my . . .

D

With a nick n

give a

This old man

he played . . .

E

nack on my . . .

H

With a nick n

give a

This old man

e played . . .

ack on my . . .

ST

With a nick r

give a

This old man

he played . . .

N

nack up to . . .

HE

With a nick n

give a

This old man

e played . . .

T

ack on my . . .

G

With a nick

give a

This old man

e played . . .

E

ack on my . . .

L

With a nick

give a

This old man

he played . . .

N

hack on my . . .

H

With a nick n

give a

This old man

THIS OLD MAN

This old man,
He played ONE,
He played nick nack on my DRUM.
Chorus:
With a nick nack Paddy whack,
Give a dog a bone,
This old man came rolling home.

This old man,
He played TWO,
He played nick nack on my SHOE.
Chorus

This old man,
He played THREE,
He played nick nack on my KNEE.
Chorus

This old man,
He played FOUR,
He played nick nack on my DOOR.
Chorus

This old man,
He played FIVE,
He played nick nack on my HIVE.
Chorus

This old man,
He played SIX,
He played nick nack on my STICKS.
Chorus

This old man,
He played SEVEN,
He played nick nack up to HEAVEN.
Chorus

This old man,
He played EIGHT,
He played nick nack on my GATE.
Chorus

This old man,
He played NINE,
He played nick nack on my LINE.
Chorus

This old man,
He played TEN,
He played nick nack on my HEN.
Chorus

POCKET ON NEXT PAGE